LAURENT DE BRUNHOFF
BABAR
and the Succotash Bird

Harry N. Abrams, Inc., Publishers

Night had fallen in Celesteville. All Babar's children were asleep, except Alexander, who rose from bed and walked to the terrace to look at the moon.

But it was not the moon giving the bright light that filled the sky. It was a beautiful bird with sparkling colors. Gliding closer, the bird started to clap his beak.

"Tash! Succotash! What are you doing here so late?"

"I can't sleep," said Alexander.

"Well, let's have some fun then. I'm a wizard. Would you like to play parachute or swing-swing?"

"What does that mean?" asked Alexander.

"You will see, little elephant, when you choose." Alexander chose swing-swing.

In a second he was floating in the air, swinging pleasantly back and forth, left and right. "Amazing! You really are a wizard!" cried Alexander. "Can you also make me fly?"

"Not now," said the bird. "Now you should go to sleep."

"Oh! But you'll come back again, right?" asked Alexander.

"I might. I like to make you happy. But remember, there are good and bad wizards, and sometimes it's hard to tell friend from foe. 'Til next time. Good-bye! Succotash! Succotash!"

Very excited, Alexander woke his brother and sisters.
He told them he had seen a magic bird. "A magic bird!"
Flora said. "You were dreaming!"

"No, it's true! He made me float in the air!"

"Oh, go back to bed!" cried Pom.

The following day the whole family went hiking in the mountains. Little Isabelle was ahead, she loved to be first. Flora and Alexander followed Celeste, but Pom was dragging along, behind Babar. Suddenly the sky grew dark and it started to rain. They rushed into a cave for shelter.

The shower was brief and the family left the cave soon. But as they did, a big bird flew out of the cave over their heads, clapping his beak and crying, "Succotash! Succotash!"

"That's my wizard!" cried Alexander. He ran downhill, following the bird.

"Alexander! Come back!" shouted Babar and Celeste. But he was already far away.

Alexander ran and ran, until the bird landed. "Why aren't you red and gold this morning?" the little elephant asked. The bird looked at him. Then he said with a smile, "That is my evening outfit, so I shine like a star."

"Can we play again?" asked Alexander.

"Of course. I can make you big or small. Which do you want?"

"Big! Big as a tree!"

"Succotash!" cried the bird waving his wings. Alexander
started to swell. He got bigger . . . and bigger and bigger!
He was taller than a pine tree.
    But still he got bigger.

Now he was as big as a mountain. He could barely see his family down below. "Stop! Stop!" he cried in horror. "I changed my mind, make me small!"

Immediately, Alexander dropped to the ground like a stone. He was smaller than a squirrel. So small that he had to look up to see the flowers.

Then he saw a beaver and thought it was a monster.
He fell backwards into a lake!
    Poor Alexander. The fish looked like whales. Where
was the wizard?

Luckily, a frog noticed him in the water and pulled him onto a lily pad. He rowed Alexander to land and said kindly, "The dragonfly will lead you to your parents."

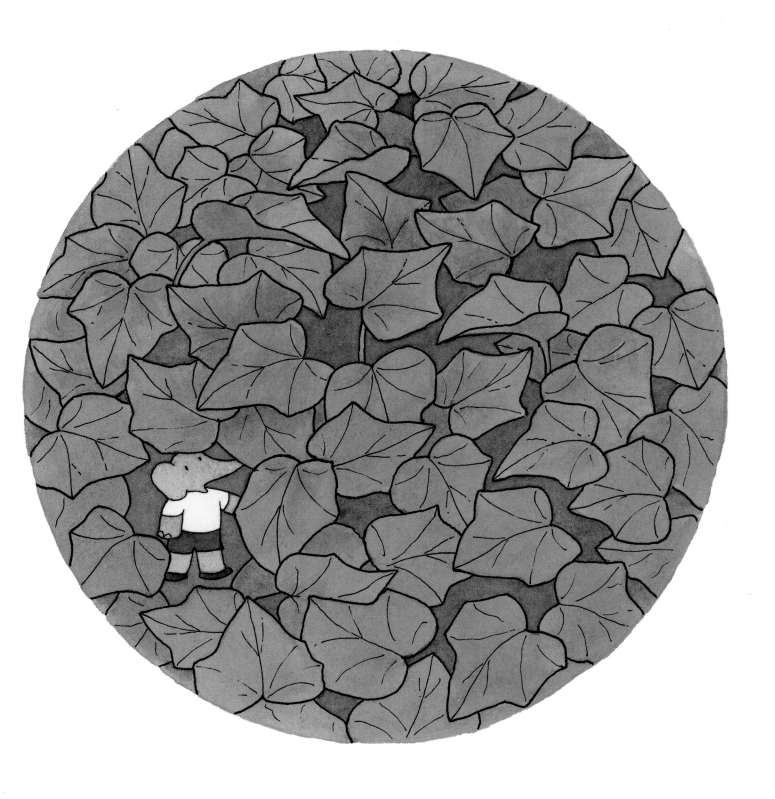

But Alexander got lost in an ivy forest. He could not see his guide anymore. "Oh, Mom and Dad, where are you?" he cried.

Meanwhile Babar, Celeste, Pom, Flora, and Isabelle were all looking for him. They searched behind every bush and every rock shouting, "Alexander! Alexander!" Babar had called his wise friend Cornelius, who was airlifted immediately. His helicopter was searching from up high in the sky.

Celeste sat on a rock in despair. "Where are you my little boy?" she sighed.

"Mommy! Here!" he cried, pulling on her shirt.

Celeste tried not to show how scared she was. She picked him up gently. "Babar! Cornelius! I've found him! Come quick!"

Alexander hardly had time to explain what had happened when they heard "Tash! Succotash!" Two birds were fighting overhead.

"Aha!" cried Cornelius. "Your wizard did not change his clothes, Alexander. There are two birds! Both cry 'Succotash!' That is what confused you."

Brown and yellow feathers fell to the ground.

"Succotash!" the good wizard cried. "What have you done now? Shame on you! You never stop making trouble! You disgrace all us wizards. Turn Alexander back to the size he was, or I'll turn you into a pile of feathers."

"It was just a joke," whined the mischief-maker.

And ZIP! Alexander was his size again. Everybody hugged him and kissed him.

"I'm going to make you small for a while," the good wizard scolded the rascal, "so you'll see how it feels. I hope, for your sake, a cat doesn't eat you."

The bird shrank to the size of a mouse and nobody could hear his miserable squawk. The golden wizard then said good-bye to everyone. "Remember, Alexander, don't jump to conclusions. There's more than one bird who can call 'Succotash!' That is how life is—right mixed with wrong. Like succotash: lima beans cooked up with corn."

Very tired, the elephants walked back to Celesteville.

That night, on the terrace, Pom, Flora, Alexander, and little Isabelle looked up at the stars. Each secretly hoped the golden bird would return and take them on a magical flight through the sky.

ARTIST'S NOTE

Ideas come to me like in a dream. I take my pencil and write little notes, draw some little sketches. My inspiration is always very visual. When the story gets in shape I start figuring out the book, how to develop the suspense and where the double-page spreads will take place. Then I draw a dummy with color studies for each page. Now, after a very precise pencil drawing of the illustration, I am ready to do the final art, page after page with watercolor. The black line comes on top of it, the final touch.

— Laurent de Brunhoff

EDITOR: Howard W. Reeves
DESIGNER: Michael J. Walsh

Library of Congress Cataloging-in-Publication Data

Brunhoff, Laurent de.
      Babar and the succotash bird / Laurent de Brunhoff.
          p. cm.
      Summary: A beautiful bird with sparkling colors and magical
powers visits Babar's son, Alexander, in the middle of the night.
      ISBN 0-8109-5700-0
      [1. Birds—Fiction. 2. Wizards—Fiction.] I. Title.
      PZ7.B82843 Baaj 2000
      [E]—dc21   00-21031

PRINTED AND BOUND IN BELGIUM

Harry N. Abrams, Inc.
100 Fifth Avenue
New York, N.Y. 10011
www.abramsbooks.com